Xcalibur's

Book 1

Xcalibur's Arena

Adventure

Charlie Krausse

illustrated by Allen D. Bayuk

To order additional copies of this book, contact:
Xlibris Corporation
1-888-795-4274
www.Xlibris.com
Orders@Xlibris.com

Author   Charlie Krausse
Illustrator   Allen D. Bayuk
Editor   Ann McCormick

Follow us on Facebook - Xcalibur's Adventure

For Luke, Maggie & Shane Krausse;
Jackson, Truman, Carter & Harrison Bayuk

The once powerful and honorable King Dragonhart lay on his bed. Many years ago, the leader of the Kingdom of Arcadia freed his people from the tyrannical reign of Lord Denomous. During their epic battle the king had two great victories and one horrific defeat. Before the Battle of Arcadia had ended, the King's wife, Queen Roselyn, gave birth to their daughter Princess Jocelyn. However, during childbirth, the queen did not survive.

Later that same year, King Dragonhart was able slay his slithery arch-enemy.

In the years to come, King Dragonhart ruled the peaceful lands of Arcadia and the people respected their king. He created a knighthood from among the finest citizens across the country. If the countryman could pass a series of tests he would then kneel before the king and receive the oath of knighthood.

However, these tests were rigorous and challenging. First, contestants would climb to the top of Mount Trollbottom; which was named simply because trolls lived in the base of the mountain guarding it from all who passed. Assuming the citizen could reach the summit, he would then advance to the next test.

6

The second qualifying test was that of archery. The contest was challenging and placed a group of citizens in a domed atmosphere with shields and protection. While the archers swarmed the arena trying to elude the others, they attempted to hit their opponents by striking a blow with their bow and arrow. The archers with the most hits qualified for the next level to become a knight.

The third test measured a person's wit, knowledge and sense of direction. The competitors entered the labyrinth, a sprawling and intricate maze. Some citizens would walk the maze for days unable to find its perplexing exits. Others gave up due to the insanity it brought them. There were even fewer who climbed the mountain or outshot the other archers who advanced past the labyrinth.

The first three levels of competition were all settled on land. The fourth was accomplished on water. Each of the remaining contestants was given a small boat to maneuver on Lake Rannoch. Making it unlike any other body of water in Arcadia for many years ago the wicked witch Orinda cast a spell on the entire lake. The spell was creative and effective; whenever two or more boats entered the water at the same time, they would crash, usually causing the boats and their crew to sink into the icy waters. The contestants knew this challenge was more dangerous than any other. The objective of this quest was to return to the dock less waterlogged than any other competing for the privilege of becoming a knight. Most of the time, champions arrived soaked and drenched from Orinda's spell and none advanced; but there were a few.

After this was the final and most difficult challenge, the gauntlet. The gauntlet consisted of an obstacle course run by the final surviving contestants. If they could dodge swaying swords and boulders intended to knock them off the plank they would bestowed as a knight. Few contestants qualified this far and most returned home cut, battered and bruised failing to become a knight.

At the beginning of the challenge, thousands began their quest to become a Knight of Arcadia. At the end, only ten were granted this high honor. And of the ten, the most outstanding were Xcalibur and Xander, brothers who survived all five competitions side-by-side.

King Dragonhart had his ten most trusted knights by his side, but needed to determine a hierarchy of power. Therefore, these knights competed against one another to establish their ranking. The knight's final challenge again was running the gauntlet but this time a mannequin queen was to be rescued from a fiery red dragon. Xcalibur and Xander agreed to work together throughout the final test and decided it would be fate who would determine king's most valued knight.

During a key battle, Xander lost control of his sword and was about to perish by the red dragon. Though, by throwing himself in front of the face of the dragon, it was Xcalibur's courage that saved Xander from the horror of the beast. Xcalibur survived but was bitten and bloody as Xander escaped with no injuries.

The two brothers rescued the mannequin queen and began exiting from the dragon's den. It was at this point that Xander's greed seized the opportunity. As they were about to exit the cave, with their reward in hand, Xander threw a rock into the darkness which caused a small rumbling noise. Xander exclaimed to his brother that the dragon was approaching. Xcalibur drew his sword and returned to the darkness. At this moment, Xander sprinted to the mouth of the cave clutching the trophy, whispering the words "sorry brother" before he left abandoned Xcalibur.

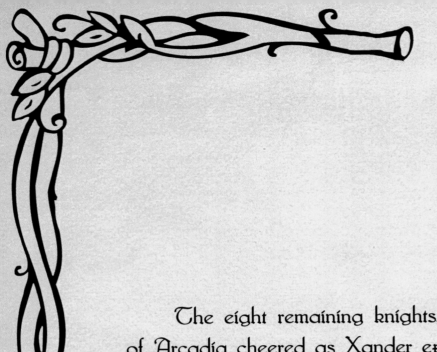

The eight remaining knights, the king and the citizens of Arcadia cheered as Xander exited the cave grasping the mannequin. Minutes later Xcalibur appeared with the expression of shock and disbelief on his face. The majority of the people celebrated as Xcalibur tended to his wounds and analyzed his uneasy situation.

Suddenly an old face from the brother's past arrived. It was Magus the mystical sorcerer. He approached King Dragonhart and the two walked in private over to a small stream. Magus waved his arms and images of Xcalibur's acts of bravery were shown and Xander's acts of deception were revealed. From this revelation, the King announced that Xcalibur would be the true and rightful winner!

As one of the honors for becoming King Dragonhart's premier knight,

21

Xcalibur was allowed to name the challenges he had won;
he called them – Xcalibur's Arena.

Times were good in Arcadia, the king had his court of knights by his side and his daughter, Princess Jocelyn, grew more and more beautiful each year. However, part of his heart was still lonely. One day, he finally decided to wed. He searched the maidens throughout the lands but none could find a place in his heart as did Queen Roselyn.

In a nearby land lived a vixen named Lady of Villainous. She was as shrewd as she was sly. It was she who pursued King Dragonhart, although her intentions were not pure from the heart. She knew if she was to wed the king then one day she would assume the throne of the almighty Kingdom of Arcadia.

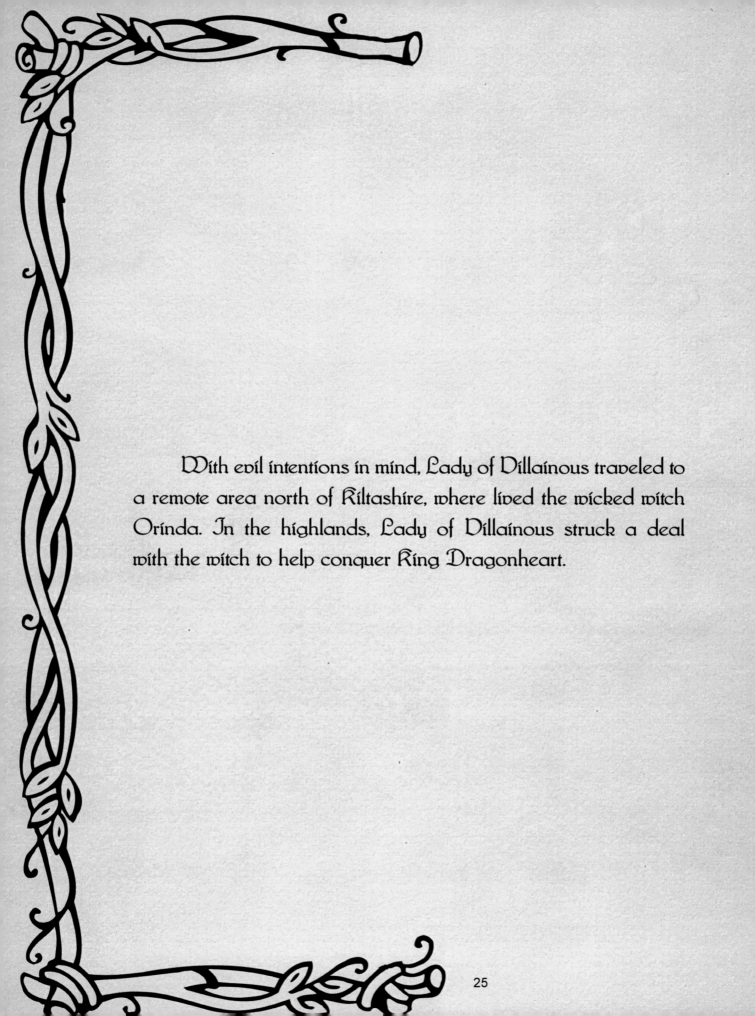

With evil intentions in mind, Lady of Dillainous traveled to a remote area north of Kiltashire, where lived the wicked witch Orinda. In the highlands, Lady of Dillainous struck a deal with the witch to help conquer King Dragonheart.

Lady of Dillainous arranged for a chance encounter with the king by help of Orinda. Orinda created a terrible storm that trapped Lady of Dillainous as King Dragonhart was traveling through the countryside. In his most noble manner, the king jumped out of his carriage and saved what he thought was a damsel in distress. As their eyes met, the evil magic of Orinda vapored from Lady of Dillainous' eyes and into King Dragonhart's eyes. This wicked spell made the King fall in love with the treacherous vixen.

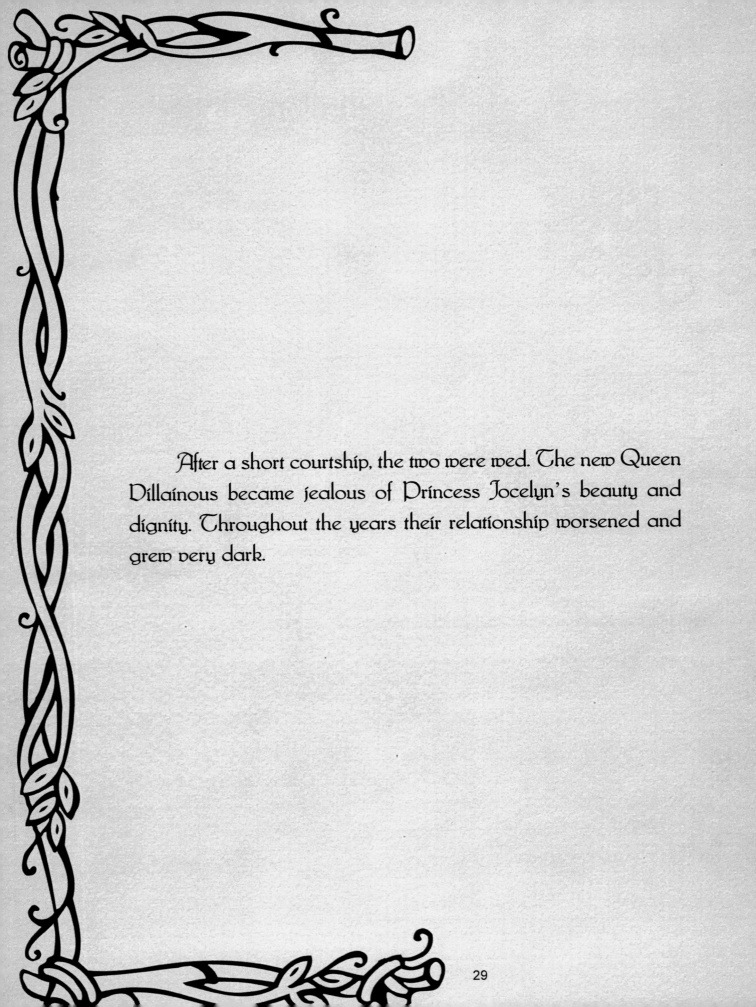

After a short courtship, the two were wed. The new Queen Villainous became jealous of Princess Jocelyn's beauty and dignity. Throughout the years their relationship worsened and grew very dark.

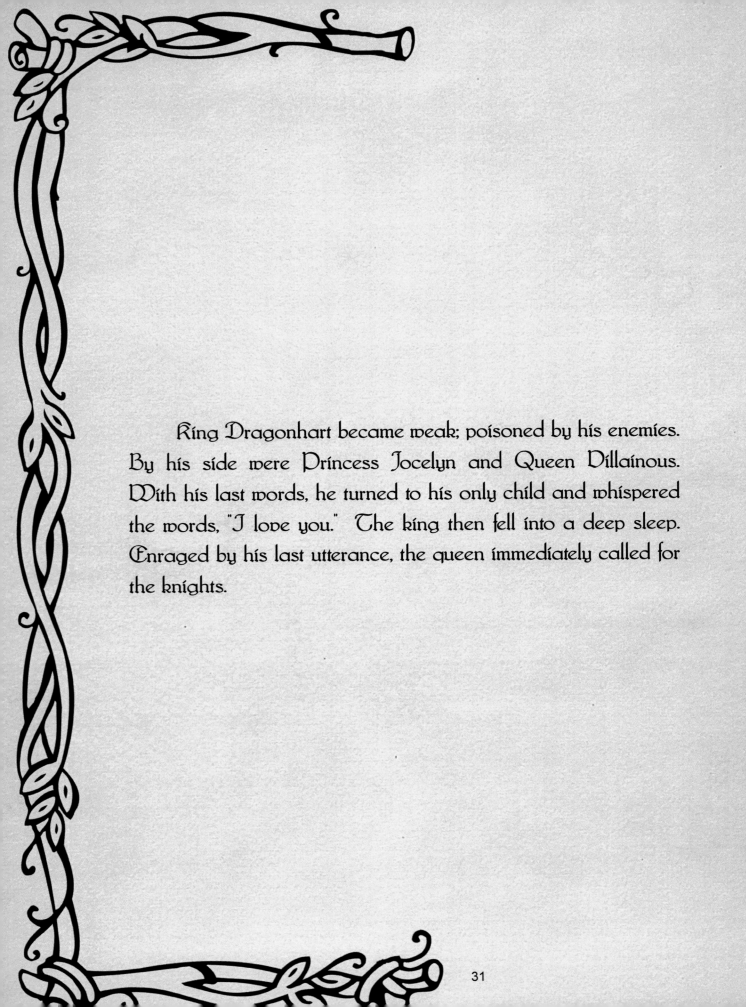

King Dragonhart became weak; poisoned by his enemies. By his side were Princess Jocelyn and Queen Villainous. With his last words, he turned to his only child and whispered the words, "I love you." The king then fell into a deep sleep. Enraged by his last utterance, the queen immediately called for the knights.

Xcalibur, Xander and the other eight arrived to discover the lifeless body of their king before them. However, the queen was not mourning the sickness of their leader, she immediately demanded that the knights take Princess Jocelyn into the dungeon and lock her there for the remainder of life.

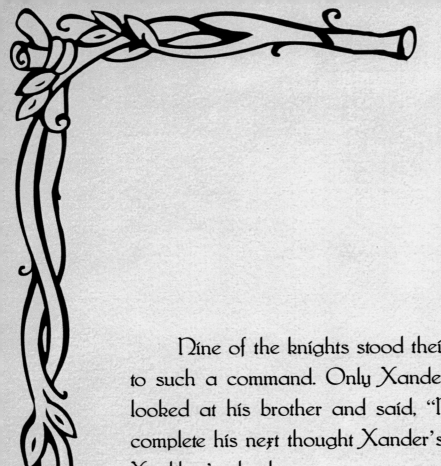

Nine of the knights stood their ground and did not react to such a command. Only Xander moved forward. Xcalibur looked at his brother and said, "No…" but before he could complete his next thought Xander's sword had been drawn to Xcalibur's cheek.

"It is my time now," stated Xander. "Your Majesty, if you would." With that the queen opened a secret door in the tower where Orinda appeared. Orinda released a spell freezing the other eight knights. Before the spell could take full effect on Xcalibur, he jumped out the window into the lake below. Princess Jocelyn screamed as she was escorted to the dungeon.

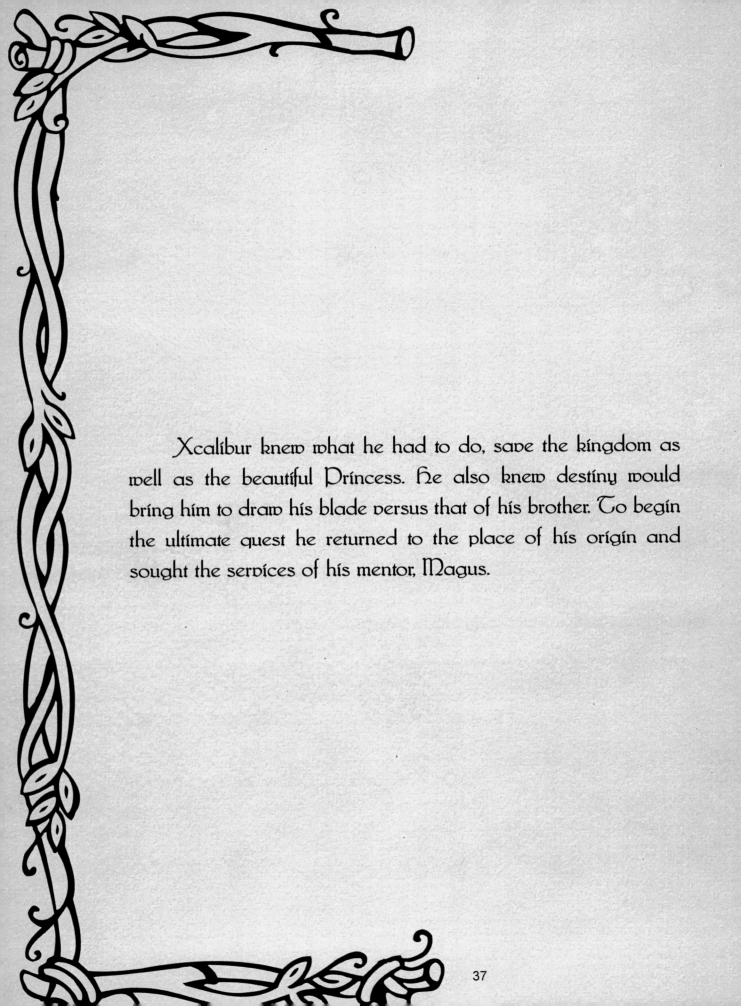

Xcalibur knew what he had to do, save the kingdom as well as the beautiful Princess. He also knew destiny would bring him to draw his blade versus that of his brother. To begin the ultimate quest he returned to the place of his origin and sought the services of his mentor, Magus.

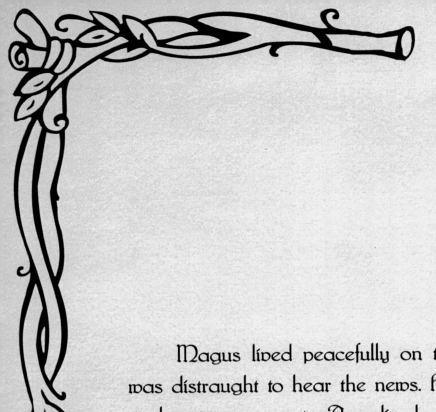

Magus lived peacefully on the edge of the forest and was distraught to hear the news. He agreed to help Xcalibur and restore peace to Arcadia, but he also knew they would need help. Deeper in the woods lived the elves; there they could find help. Magus and Xcalibur approached the leader of the elves, Jayden. The elves remained neutral in almost all situations unless an act of vengeance was perpetrated in their lands. Xcalibur related his story and the grand elf listened. After digesting his visitor's words, Jayden decided to send Aurick, his best archer, along to help restore peace in the kingdom.

While Xcalibur was seeking help from his friends, the queen had assembled her own Army of Evil. She knew Xcalibur would return and she was ready.

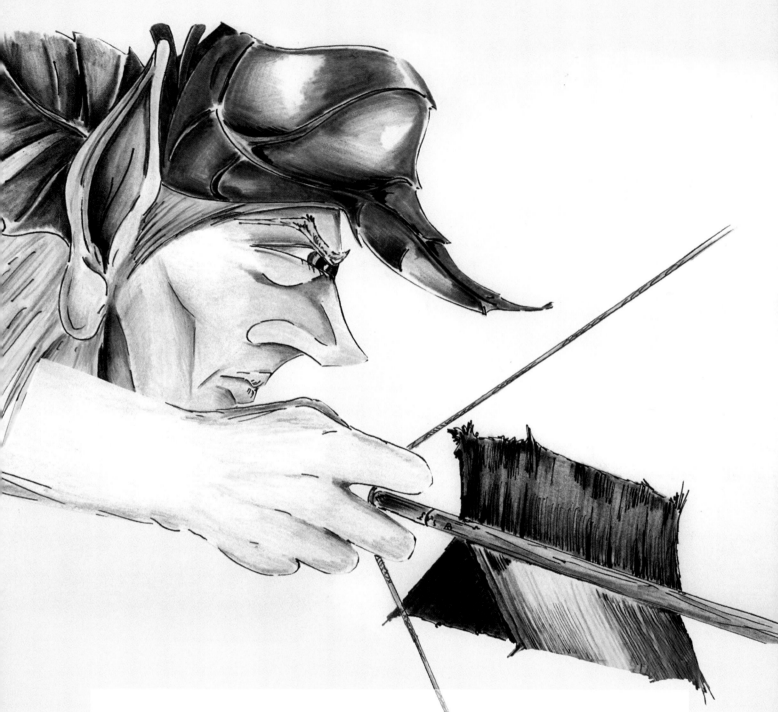

The fateful date arrived. The small heroic group of three approached the castle once powerfully ruled by the great King Dragonhart. Perched on the watchtower, a group of the queen's guards surveyed the grounds. Aurick eliminated all guards with his deadly accurate bow and arrow.

As Xcalibur and Aurick battled more of the Army of Darkness, Magus separated from his companions.

One of the more valuable powers in being a sorcerer was the ability to detect the presence of other magicians. His mission was to search out and locate Orinda.

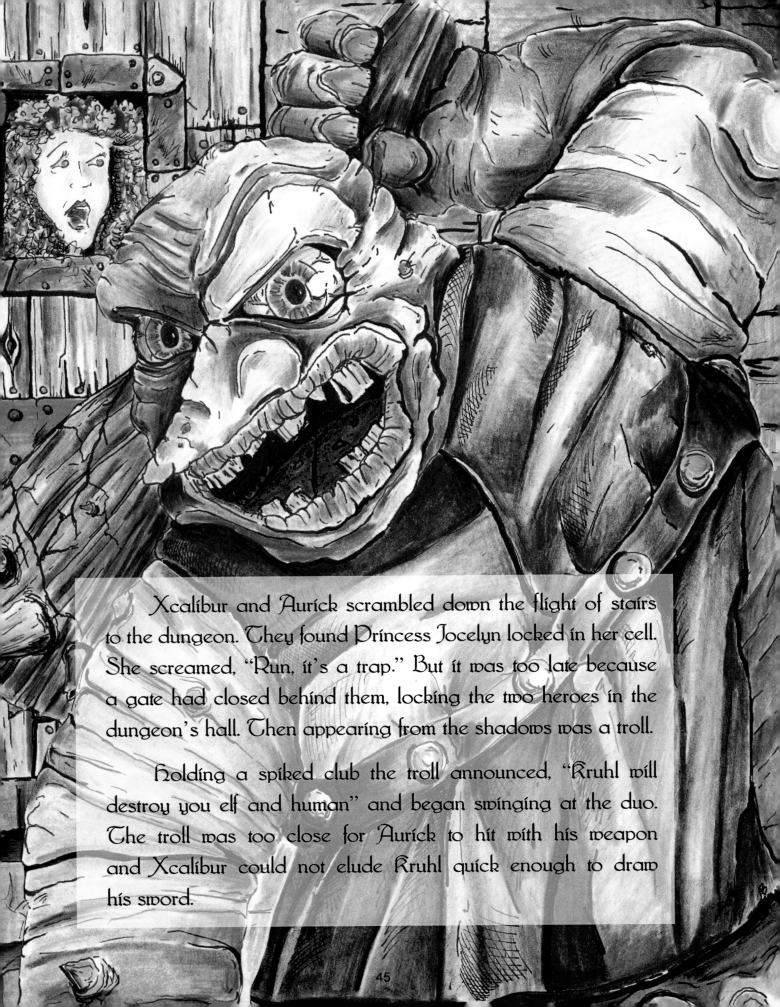

Xcalibur and Aurick scrambled down the flight of stairs to the dungeon. They found Princess Jocelyn locked in her cell. She screamed, "Run, it's a trap." But it was too late because a gate had closed behind them, locking the two heroes in the dungeon's hall. Then appearing from the shadows was a troll.

Holding a spiked club the troll announced, "Kruhl will destroy you elf and human" and began swinging at the duo. The troll was too close for Aurick to hit with his weapon and Xcalibur could not elude Kruhl quick enough to draw his sword.

Then Xcalibur heard familiar laughter from the shadows. It was Xander with sword already drawn. "Brother, you should not have returned. You will now become a lifelong prisoner like the princess before you."

Xcalibur rolled out of the way from a massive club strike from the troll, sprung to his feet, and drew his sword, locking blades with Xander.

A few levels above Magus stood waiting for the wicked witch Orinda. Suddenly huge gusts of wind stormed through the hallway. Placing his hands stretched out, Magus blocked the wicked winds then countered by creating a giant fog in the room, not allowing Orinda to see her enemy. From there Magus was able to dull Orinda's motions with a spell of his own. The witch was now moving more slowly than normal speed, enabling Magus to capture her.

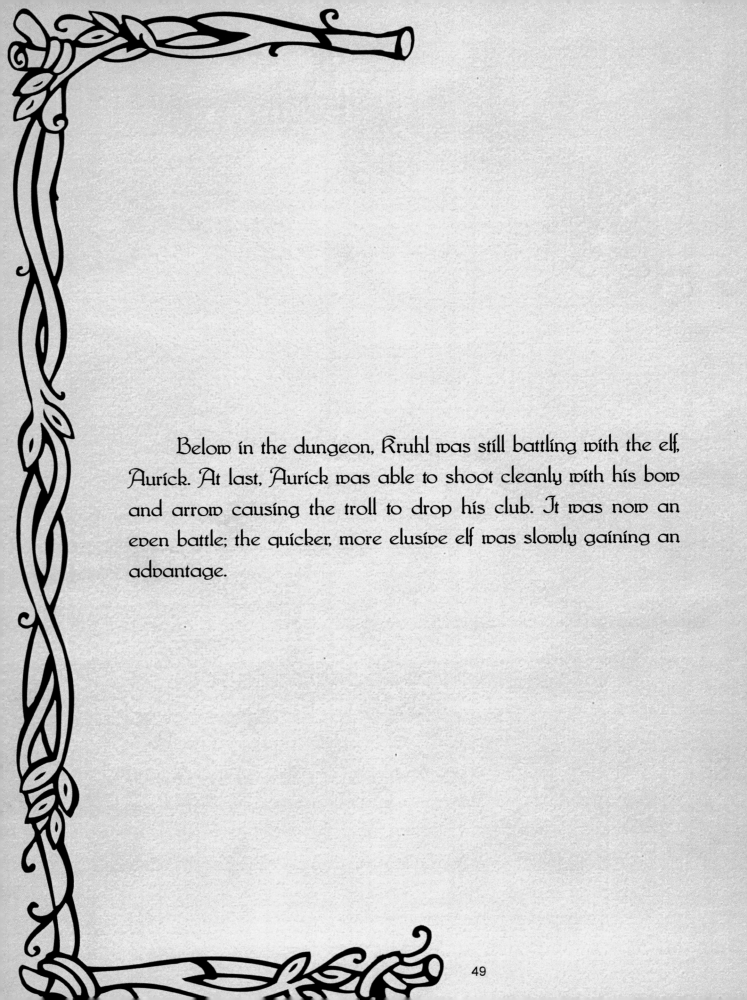

Below in the dungeon, Kruhl was still battling with the elf, Aurick. At last, Aurick was able to shoot cleanly with his bow and arrow causing the troll to drop his club. It was now an even battle; the quicker, more elusive elf was slowly gaining an advantage.

The two brothers circled each other, neither making the first move; both ready to strike. Finally, Xander's rage shattered the silence and the battle began. The brothers fought back and forth gaining and losing advantage as they battled their way throughout the dungeon.

As the siblings were locking swords, Aurick grabbed the keys to the cell and tossed them to the princess. She was able to free herself and jumped on the back of the troll, trying to help her new friend, Aurick.

The swords of Xcalibur and Xander crashed together again and again. During one of their strikes they broke an oil lamp that drenched both swords and ignited a blade of fire in each combatant's hand.

After many rounds of blades crossing both in fiery blaze and with out, Xcalibur knocked the sword from Xander's hand and dropped him to his knees.

Magus raised the gate of the closed dungeon's entrance with Orinda still imprisoned. Suddenly, appearing from a secret passage was the queen. More devious as ever she sought to end Xcalibur with one final blow with Xander's sword. Witnessing the queen's evil actions, Princess Jocelyn grabbed Kruhl's club and flung it at her evil stepmother. This act caught the wicked vixen off guard. She dropped the sword, fell to the ground, and broke into tears.

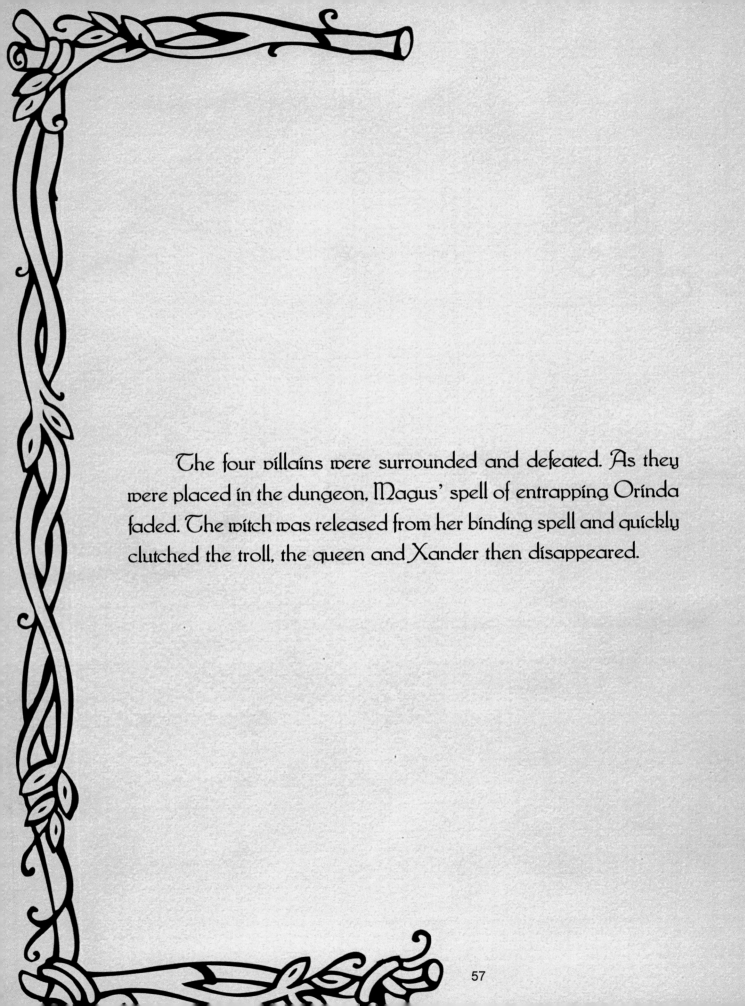

The four villains were surrounded and defeated. As they were placed in the dungeon, Magus' spell of entrapping Orinda faded. The witch was released from her binding spell and quickly clutched the troll, the queen and Xander then disappeared.

The evil doers may have escaped, but the question that loomed on everyone's mind was how do they save the king. Magus replied, "You must retrieve the Elements of Arcadia."

The battle had been won. The princess had been saved. The kingdom was restored. A new alliance was formed. But the story is just beginning.

Edwards Brothers,Inc!
Thorofare, NJ 08086
19 November, 2010
BA2010324